W9-DFD-871

GREENUP COUNTY PUBLIC LIBRARY
614 MAIN STREET
GREENUP, KY 41144

KLOOZ
Clues in the
Car Wash

by J. Banscherus
translated by Daniel C. Baron
illustrated by Ralf Butschkow

Librarian Reviewer
Marci Peschke
Librarian, Dallas Independent School District
MA Education Reading Specialist, Stephen F. Austin State University
Learning Resources Endorsement, Texas Women's University

Reading Consultant
Mary Evenson
Middle School Teacher, Edina Public Schools, MN
MA in Education, University of Minnesota

STONE ARCH BOOKS
Minneapolis   San Diego

First published in the United States in 2007
by Stone Arch Books,
151 Good Counsel Drive, P.O. Box 669,
Mankato, Minnesota 56002
www.stonearchbooks.com

First published by Arena Books,
Rottendorfer str. 16, D-97074,
Würzburg, Germany

Copyright © 2002 Jürgen Banscherus
Illustrations copyright © 2002 Ralf Butschkow

All rights reserved. No part of this publication may be reproduced
in whole or in part, or stored in a retrieval system, or transmitted
in any form or by any means, electronic, mechanical, photocopying,
recording, or otherwise, without written permission of the publisher.

Library of Congress Cataloging-in-Publication Data
Banscherus, Jürgen.
    [Faule Tricks und nasse Füsse]
    Clues in the Car Wash / by J. Banscherus; translated by Daniel C.
Baron; illustrated by Ralf Butschkow.
    p. cm. — (Pathway Books – Klooz)
    First published: Würzburg, Germany: Arena Books, 2002.
    Summary: Olga hires fifth-grade detective Klooz to find out how
her precious car got scratched at the car wash on Main Street.
    ISBN-13: 978-1-59889-337-3 (library binding)
    ISBN-10: 1-59889-337-8 (library binding)
    ISBN-13: 978-1-59889-432-5 (paperback)
    ISBN-10: 1-59889-432-3 (paperback)
    [1. Automobiles—Fiction. 2. Car washes—Fiction. 3. Swindlers and
swindling—Fiction. 4. Mystery and detective stories.] I. Butschkow, Ralf,
ill. II. Baron, Daniel C. III. Title.
PZ7.B22927Clu 2007
[Fic]—dc22   2006027359

Art Director: Heather Kindseth
Graphic Designer: Kay Fraser

1 2 3 4 5 6 12 11 10 09 08 07

Printed in the United States of America

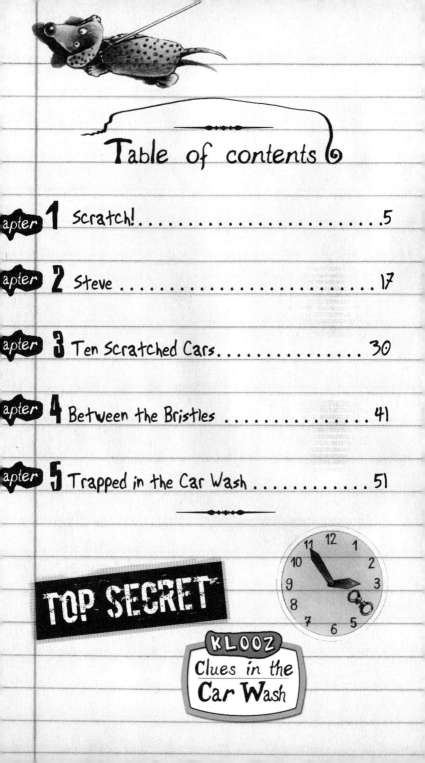

Table of contents

TOP SECRET

KLOOZ
Clues in the
Car Wash

CHAPTER 1

Scratch!

Detectives don't make a lot of money, especially if the detective is a kid.

I charge my customers five packs of Carpenter's chewing gum. When you only get three dollars a week for your allowance, you can forget about buying anything big.

I've been thinking how useful a computer could be in my line of business.

That's why, every chance I get, I bug my mom to buy me a computer. I even promised to wash the dinner dishes for the next twenty years.

"There are two reasons for not getting a computer," she said. "First, you would spend all day playing games and shooting at monsters."

No Video games with monsters

NO!

Monsters are people too

No m in

"And second?" I asked.

"And second, we can't afford it."

I could have explained to my mother that I wouldn't sit at the computer all day shooting monsters. After all, I didn't need the computer for playing games. I needed it for my cases.

Mom had a point with her second reason, though. Ever since my dad left, we have to count every penny.

But I don't give up easily.

I thought it over for quite a while.

Two days and six pieces of chewing gum later I had an idea of how I could get a computer.

First I visited the local baker around the corner. I told him I could deliver fresh baked bread every morning to his customers. But the baker just shook his head.

"I am sorry, Klooz. I can't hire kids. Those are the boss's rules. I could get into trouble," he said.

In the office of the *Daily News* it was the same story.

"You want to deliver newspapers?" asked a guy with tons of hair gel dripping from his head. "In a couple of years we could use you, but you're just too young right now."

Every place I tried, they said the same things. "You're too young." "We could get into trouble." "We don't hire kids."

I didn't want to deliver diamonds or secret rocket plans! I just wanted to deliver a few loaves of bread or some newspapers. Why was that such a problem?

As always, when I hit a roadblock, I
visited Olga. I always bought my chewing
gum at her newspaper stand. She had
helped me many times before, and not just
with my cases.

She gave me a can of cola and asked, "Is something wrong, Klooz?"

"Yup," I answered.

"A new case?" she asked.

I nodded, took a drink, and put a piece of chewing gum in my mouth. Then I told Olga all the things that I had been through in the last couple of days. She didn't interrupt me.

When I was finally finished, she said, "I would love to hire you, sweetie."

I hate it when she calls me "sweetie."

"But I am barely making ends meet myself," she said.

"That's okay," I said.

I started to leave.

Olga grabbed me by the arm.

"Come to think of it," she said, "I do have a case for you."

A case? That would be perfect! If no one would give me a steady job, I could work as a detective. Klooz on the case.

"Tell me all about it," I said.

"Look at my car," Olga said. "Just look at it!"

As usual, she had parked her car on the other side of the street where she could keep an eye on it.

She loves that car as if it were a member of her family. The car was freshly washed and the chrome bumper gleamed in the sunshine.

"Yeah, it sure is a beauty," I said.

"Are you blind?" she yelled. "The driver's door, Klooz! The driver's door!"

I took a closer look and saw the damage. There was an ugly scratch the whole length of the driver's door.

"Isn't that awful?" asked Olga as I stood in front of her newspaper stand. She had tears in her eyes.

"Who did that?" I asked.

Olga noisily blew her nose into her gigantic flowered hankie.

"I don't know, Klooz, but when I find the person who did it . . . !" She swallowed. "Will you take the case?"

I nodded.

"The usual fee?" she asked.

I nodded.

She beamed a huge smile at me.

"When did you first notice the scratch?" I asked.

Olga thought for a minute. "Yesterday, right after I drove it to the car wash."

"You don't wash your car by hand?" I asked in amazement.

I always thought that since Olga loved her car so much, she had a special bathtub for her car, one with a whirlpool and a rubber ducky.

"It was an exception," she explained. "I was invited to a birthday party and so I had to have a clean car. And I was in a hurry."

If I let her keep talking, she would tell me what they had to eat at the party and what each person wore.

"Which car wash did you go to?" I asked.

"The one on Main Street. The owner is a customer of mine."

"Who isn't?" I said, smiling.

Olga grinned and pinched my cheek. I hate it when she does that.

CHAPTER 2

Steve

The gas station on Main Street was on my way to school. Every now and then I buy a bag of chips there.

The other kids in my class who go there buy candy bars, but I don't touch those. Ever since I solved a mystery with rats and a chocolate Christmas cake, I know that sweet stuff just doesn't agree with me.

On this particular afternoon there wasn't much going on at the gas station on Main Street. There was only one car at the twelve gas pumps. Two other cars were waiting in line for the car wash.

I wasn't sure what I was looking for, so I walked around and looked for clues. I nosed around the gas pumps, stared at the ground, and peeked into the trash cans, but didn't see anything. There was nothing suspicious about the gas station.

Suddenly the door to the gas station market flew open and out popped the owner. His name is Steve, but some of his customers call him Stevie.

We kids aren't allowed to call him that, of course. In spite of the heat, Stevie was wearing a thick black ski cap on his head. He always wore that cap. He probably didn't even take it off when he slept.

"Are you looking for something?" he asked.

"Not really," I said.

"Then get lost. This isn't a playground!"

The guy was very unfriendly.

To think that at least once a week I spent some of my allowance in his store.

If Olga behaved the way he did, she would have to close her newspaper stand.

I decided that from now on I would never spend another dime at his gas station. He can keep his stupid chips and candy bars!

I was about to leave when a man came running up to us from the car wash.

His face was bright red.

He stood in front of Stevie and gasped for breath.

"My car!" he gasped.

"What's wrong with your car?" asked Stevie.

"The paint!" the man cried.

"Yeah?" asked Stevie.

"It has a scratch!" the man replied.

Stevie pushed his ski cap back a little.

"Lots of cars have scratches," he said.

When he spoke with adults, he could sound friendly. "I have little bottles of touch-up paint in my garage," said Stevie.

"I don't want any touch-up paint!" roared the man.

His face was so
red that a tomato
would have
looked pink
next to him.
"Something is
wrong with your
car wash and you have
to pay for the damage!"

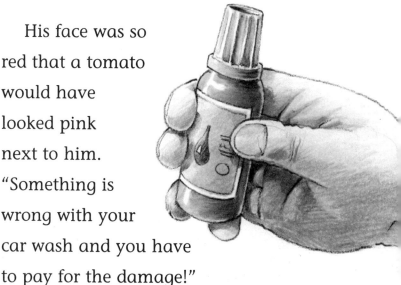

"Not so fast," said Stevie. "What makes
you think my car wash scratched your
car? Maybe someone did it last night."

"Last night my car was parked in a
locked garage!"

"Well, let's take a look at this
scratch," Stevie said.

The man's station wagon was parked
in front of the car wash, gleaming in the
bright sun.

A deep scratch was on the driver's door. It looked exactly like the scratch on Olga's car.

Stevie scratched his ear. "That doesn't look too good," he said.

"Doesn't look too good?" the man said. "The whole door has to be repainted!"

"Maybe not," said Stevie. "With my touch-up paint it can look as good as new."

Just then, Stevie remembered that I had been standing there the whole time.

"You're still here?" he snapped at me. "Get lost! And make it quick!"

It's really a shame that I couldn't stick around to see what happened next. Stevie gave me such a dirty look that I thought I better go.

After walking a couple of blocks down Main Street, I turned around.

Stevie and the driver had stopped arguing. The customer got back into his car and drove off, squealing his tires.

A few minutes later I was back at Olga's newsstand. She was in the middle of selling a pack of Carpenter's chewing gum to a nicely dressed man with an expensive briefcase.

Classy people have good taste.

"How's it going, sweetie?" she asked.

I wiped some fake sweat from my forehead and sighed. This trick always works.

"It sure is hot today, isn't it?" asked Olga. "Would you like some cola?"

What did I tell you? Hmmm. Maybe I could make more money as an actor instead of a detective. After Olga handed me a can, I told her what I had seen at Stevie's gas station.

There was silence for a while. Olga sucked on a piece of candy, while I bathed my tongue in my free cola.

"Maybe it was just a weird coincidence," Olga said after hearing my report.

"Maybe," I said. "Or maybe you were right. Maybe something is wrong with the car wash."

I drank my soda pop, chewed my gum, and thought it over. I got it!

"You can help me, Olga," I said.

"Gladly, sweetie," Olga replied. "But what can I do?"

"Tomorrow you have to go through the car wash again," I said.

Olga's candy fell from her mouth. She gasped for breath.

"And I will go with you," I said.

"No!" Olga said emphatically. "No, no, no! One scratch is enough!"

"What's one more scratch when you already have one?" I asked. "Besides, the door has to be repainted anyway. Or did Stevie sell you one of his bottles of touch-up paint?"

"He tried. But I only let experts take care of my darling car," she replied. She stared at her car. "Okay, kid, I'll go, but if my baby is all scratched up afterward, you're going to pay the bill."

"It's a deal," I said. "What time should we meet?"

"Come by around five o'clock. I'll close the stand a little early tomorrow."

"Thanks, Olga!" I said.

I told you she was a great friend. Who else would be willing to drive their car through the car wash a second time, and risk more damage?

CHAPTER 3

Ten Scratched Cars

At home, my mom was waiting for me.

"Dinner is at six o'clock," she said.

"I'm sorry, Mom," I said.

"Do you have a new case?" Mom asked as she served me tomato slices with cheese. I had hoped for a pizza, but my mom had decided once again that we needed to eat healthier.

"Why do you ask?" I replied.

"You look funny, like you've been thinking a lot."

Whether I look good or bad, whether I am hungry or not, whether I feel like talking or don't, my mom always thinks it's because I have a new case. I told her about Olga's scratched door.

"It's a good thing that I go to a different car wash," she said when I was finished. "Maybe there's something stuck in the brushes."

"The brushes?"

She nodded. "The brushes that rub against the cars."

"Then why did it only happen to Olga and that man?"

"I don't know," she said. "You're the detective."

In bed I thought about what my mom had said. An object stuck in the brushes. That could be it. The only question was, how did it get there? And why didn't Stevie or someone else at the garage fix the problem?

It was raining the next morning when I looked out the window. That was bad for my case. No one would want to wash a car in that kind of weather. I was soaked by the time I reached school.

As the day went on, it rained harder and harder.

I thought of calling the weatherman on TV. He obviously didn't realize how hard he was making my detective work.

After school, I ran home. I was changing out of my soaking wet clothes when the phone rang.

It was Olga. She said she had to see me right away.

"I haven't even eaten yet," I told her.

"You can eat later!" she said.

"What's the rush?" I asked.

"It's about the scratch, Klooz!"

I ate a yogurt as fast as I could.

Then I headed for Olga's.

It was still raining, and for the third time on the same day I got soaking wet. I looked for scratches on every car that I passed, but saw none.

When I finally reached Olga's newsstand, there were two women there, standing under umbrellas. One of the women was tall and skinny and the other one was short and plump.

"This is the detective I was telling you about," Olga introduced me.

The tall woman looked me over. I was dripping wet and my shoes squeaked whenever I took a step.

"You can't be serious," she said to Olga.

"I am very serious!" Olga replied. "You won't find a better detective in the whole city." Then Olga turned to me and said, "Both of their doors were scratched."

"At the car wash on Main Street?"

Both women nodded. "Are you really a detective?" the tall woman asked.

"Yes," I replied, and said nothing else. I got the feeling I had said enough.

"We want to hire you," said the plump woman.

"I'm already working for Olga," I said.

"You can work for all three of us," replied Olga. "Whoever scratched my car obviously made all the other scratches."

"So now I have three clients?" I asked.

"Um, actually there are ten," said Olga.

"Ten?" I shouted.

"Ten people whose driver doors were scratched in the car wash," she explained.

"How do you know that?"

"I asked every single customer yesterday," she answered.

Unbelievable! Ten doors!

"Can you close your stand right now?" I asked. "Please, Olga?"

She first looked at her wristwatch, then in her cash register. She looked at her watch again before saying, "Okay, Klooz." She closed her newspaper stand, said good-bye to the two women, and put out a closed sign.

Sorry, we're closed.
I'll be back tomorrow.

When we arrived at the gas station, it was only drizzling. We were the only ones who wanted to wash our car.

Olga paid inside the gas station and got a plastic computer card from the attendant. Outside, she stuck the card into a machine. Then she drove into the car wash until a light flashed "Stop." Then Olga put the car into neutral and leaned back into her seat.

After the car was soaped up, the giant brushes starting to spin.

Before Olga could stop me, I jumped out of the car and hid behind the arm that supported the giant brushes.

In the middle of spraying water and unbelievable noise I started hunting for clues.

I've never been so wet in all my life. It was especially bad when I stuck my arms up to my elbows in the bristles in order to find any hard or sharp objects. The bristles were incredibly soft.

The warm air that dried Olga's car was not enough to dry me, too.

So when I got back into the car I was soaking wet. Again.

"Thank goodness you're still alive!" Olga cried. "I was so worried. Hey, stop dripping on the leather seat."

I sneezed.

"I can't help it," I said. "I have just gotten a complete car wash including preclean and wax."

"You poor boy," said Olga as she drove out of the car wash.

"So what's with the bristles? Did you find anything?" she asked.

"They looked okay," I answered.

She got out of the car and looked it over. "No new scratches."

"I didn't think there would be," I said. "It's probably all just a big coincidence."

Olga nodded. "I'll drive you home."

"Achoo!"

CHAPTER 4

Between the Bristles

At home, I went straight to the bathtub, stuck two pieces of Carpenter's chewing gum in my mouth, and started thinking. There is no better place to think than in the bathtub with two fantastic pieces of chewing gum in my mouth.

Were the scratches all caused by the same thing? Was I barking up the wrong tree?

I shut my eyes and sank into the water. I let my thoughts wander over pictures in my mind.

The pictures came and went. I saw Stevie, with his unfriendly face underneath the ski cap.

I saw the giant spraying brushes. Scratched car doors. Lots and lots of scratched car doors.

I saw the upset look on Olga's face when she looked at her car. And the touch-up paint. Why touch-up paint?

I quickly jumped out of the tub and got dressed. I wasn't sure what the touch-up paint had to do with the whole case, but I felt I was on the right track.

It was the kind of thing that made an experienced detective feel a shiver run down his back. Or maybe I was getting a cold.

When I got to the gas station, almost all the pumps were being used. The sun shining on gas and oil puddles made tiny rainbows. In the station I looked for touch-up paint, but with no success. Strange.

"Can I help you?" asked the young woman behind the counter. Compared to Stevie, she was almost friendly.

"Do you have any touch-up paint?" I asked.

"Touch-up paint?" she asked back. "What do you need touch-up paint for?"

"Um, for my mom's car," I said.

"We don't sell any," replied the woman. She turned to help another customer.

There was no touch-up paint in Stevie's gas station? But Stevie had tried to sell it to Olga and that other guy. Weird. What did that mean?

At six o'clock I ate dinner with my mother. I helped her wash the dishes and then did my homework.

Then I asked, "Can I go out again?"

My mother looked at the kitchen clock. "At this hour?" she asked.

"It's important!"

"For your case?"

I nodded.

"And it's not dangerous?" she asked.

I shook my head.

"Well, okay, but be home by nine p.m.," she said.

"Nine thirty?" I asked.

"All right," she said. "Be on time."

I kissed her on the nose and walked out of the house. The gas station closed at nine o'clock. Nine thirty would be just enough time.

There was nothing going on at the gas station. There were no customers at the pumps. Stevie was standing inside by the cash register talking to the cashier.

As fast as I could I ran over to the car wash and hid behind a big garbage bin. This could take a while, I thought. I should have brought some extra chewing gum.

Just then Stevie came over and started to scrub the car wash floor with a mop. He whistled while he worked.

After about fifteen minutes he stuck his hand in his pocket and pulled out a long object.

He started to do something with the bristles on one of the brushes.

Then he walked over to the door. I thought he was going to lock it.

He must have forgotten his keys, because he walked back to the gas station, shaking his head.

This was my chance! Even if I only had a minute, I had to try something.

I ran out from my hiding place.

I raced over to the car wash and slipped through the little door in the middle of the big car wash door. I examined the brush that I had seen Stevie messing with.

Sure enough, between two bristles I found a thin screwdriver. Stevie had cleverly stuck the screwdriver in a hole where some bristles had been pulled out.

I pulled out the screwdriver and quickly ran back to my hiding place. Just in time, too. Stevie came back and locked the car wash door.

Five minutes later he drove off in his little sports car.

Deep in thought, I returned home. It was exactly nine thirty.

My mother was sitting in front of the television.

I showed her the screwdriver and said, "He does it with this."

"Who?" she asked.

"Stevie," I replied.

My mother's mouth fell open. "I don't believe it," she said.

"I saw him put this between the bristles with my own eyes," I replied.

"Why would he do that?" my mother asked.

"I'll find out tomorrow," I answered. "And I'll solve the case, or my name isn't Klooz!"

Later in bed, thoughts raced through my mind. Should I bring the evidence to the police? They would be able to prove that it was this screwdriver that scratched the car doors. But Stevie would swear up and down that he never stuck that screwdriver between the bristles. It would be his word against mine.

The police would probably believe a grown-up before they believed a kid. Maybe I needed to talk to Stevie first. But if I did, I'd better have a plan.

CHAPTER 5

Trapped in the Car Wash

The next day my class visited a museum. There were lots of broken pots, dented helmets, and rusty bracelets. It was like a very old junkyard. But it did give me lots of time to think about the case.

By the time we were riding back to school on the bus, I had made my plan. I was really quite proud of myself. If I was successful, they could make a statue of me, like the ones they have in the park.

It would have to be fifteen feet tall and a gold plaque would read "To the Greatest Detective in the City."

When I got home, I dropped my backpack in my room, ate two plates of spaghetti, and then went to see Olga. I needed her.

Without Olga, my plan wouldn't work.

"Would you like something to drink, sweetie?" she asked.

I shook my head. "Is your tank full?" I asked.

"That's a funny way to put it," said Olga. "But, yes, I am a little full from dinner."

"No, I mean your car," I said. "Is it full of gas?"

"Uh, no, it could use a little topping off," she answered.

"Close your newsstand. We're going to get gas," I said.

"But . . . !" she started to protest.

"Please, Olga," I said. "If you help me, we will know within the hour who scratched your car!"

Olga rolled her eyes and sighed. "How can I say no to the great detective?"

As we drove to the gas station, I explained what she needed to do. "Tell Stevie his sports car looks terrible, and it needs a wash. Then you'll drive back to your newsstand. Got it?"

Olga wondered what I was up to, but she agreed to do as I asked.

The gas station was pretty dead. That might not be good for business, but it was very good for us. Olga put ten dollars of gas in her tank and went inside to pay. I ran to the car wash and hid, like the day before, behind the nearby garbage bin.

I hoped Olga was talking to Stevie. He would listen to her, as one car lover to another. Now Stevie just had to play along. Yes! A few minutes later he came out of the station, got into his car, and drove toward the car wash.

He stuck a plastic card into the machine and drove into the car wash. The big door closed behind his car and the wash cycle began.

Without a second to lose, I dashed from my hiding place and ran over to the car wash.

I peered through the windows. Inside, the brushes were spinning like crazy. They were cleaning the hood, the front tires, and the bumper of Stevie's car.

Slowly, the brushes moved down the sides of the car. I counted as I waited.

21 . . . 22 . . . 23 . . .

Then I ran to the emergency stop button and pushed it.

THUNK!

At that moment the entire car wash shut off.

I had stopped the brushes just as they reached the doors.

The doors were now pinned shut. It was impossible for Stevie to get out of the car.

Klooz's auto advice: Never buy a two-door car.

Up to this point my plan had worked perfectly. Now came the most difficult part.

I stuck a piece of chewing gum in my mouth, took a deep breath, and walked into the car wash itself.

Stevie was going crazy inside his car.

I knocked on his window and made a motion that he should roll it down.

When he did, streams of water from his roof poured into the open window and onto his lap.

That made Stevie even angrier.

"You again!" he roared. "What in the world are you doing? Are you crazy? Get me out of here!"

I let him shout for a while, and then I took the screwdriver out of my pocket.

"Is this yours?" I asked as he gasped for breath.

"Of course it's mine!" he yelled as he reached out the window for it. "Give it back!"

I took a step back and smiled.

"What do you think would happen if I called the police?" I asked.

Suddenly Stevie stopped yelling.

"Who are you, anyway?" he asked me in a much quieter voice.

"Klooz," I answered. "I was hired to find out how the cars got scratched up using your car wash."

Stevie thought for a minute and said, "You're working for Olga, right?"

"Right."

"You two set a trap for me, right?"

"Right," I said again.

"It had to be Olga," Stevie mumbled. "Boy, am I in a mess!"

"I want to know why you did it," I said.

"Then you'll let me out?" Stevie asked.

"Maybe."

"And if I don't tell you?" he asked.

"I'll call the police," I said.

Stevie's face grew pale. "No police," he cried. "I'll tell you everything, but first you have to let me out of here."

He gave me a code for the car wash, and I punched the numbers into the control panel.

The car wash started working again.

Five minutes later, Stevie drove out of the car wash and then got out of his car.

"Follow me," he said.

We walked a few blocks to Stevie's house.

Then Stevie walked over to his garage and lifted the door.

There were boxes stacked all the way to the ceiling.

"In all of these boxes . . . ," he began.

"There is touch-up paint," I said, ending his sentence for him.

He nodded. A friend had brought them last year, he explained.

Perhaps they were stolen. He didn't know. In any case, he sold the touch-up paint to customers who had scratched cars and split the money with his friend.

"Where do you sell the touch-up paint?" I asked.

"In the store next to the car wash," Stevie said.

"That's practical," I said. "And because you weren't selling enough, you thought you could sell more with a little help from the screwdriver."

He nodded. "The gas station and the car wash don't make that much money. I was hoping to make a little more by selling the touch-up paint."

I thought.

Something still wasn't adding up.

"How did you make sure that only the driver's doors were scratched?" I asked.

"I tested it out on an old, junky car. Each car's door handle always knocked the screwdriver loose when the car drove through."

Clever, I thought. I asked him if he had sold more touch-up paint lately.

"Much more," he answered. "Some weeks as many as thirty bottles. Almost no one thought that the scratches came from my car wash. It was a stupid thing for me to do. I admit it."

We were silent for a little while. Then Stevie asked, "Are you going to go to the police?"

I shook my head. "My job is over. I'll talk to Olga. She'll decide what happens next."

Then he asked, "Could I have my screwdriver back?"

"Later," I said. "Maybe."

Give up the only evidence that I had? Not even a beginner would do something that dumb.

* * *

What I figured would happen, did happen.

Olga is simply too kind. She came to an agreement with Stevie. He would pay for her door to be repainted. He would also pay for the repainting of the other ten car doors that Olga knew about.

Stevie offered to do the job himself with touch-up paint, but everyone refused. They wanted expert painters to do the repair work.

Stevie's agreement with Olga cost him a bundle of cash. He lost all the money he made selling touch-up paint because of the repair bills.

I didn't feel sorry for Stevie at all. He deserved everything he got.

Three days after solving the case, I visited Olga. Her old car with its new paint gleamed in the sunlight.

"I haven't paid you yet," she said as she pushed five packs of chewing gum across the counter.

She also handed me an envelope.

I opened it and four fifty-dollar bills fell out. Two hundred dollars!

"Is that for me?" I stuttered.

Olga nodded. "I took up a collection from the people whose cars were scratched."

Wow! A few more cases like this one, and I would be able to buy a computer.

"Olga, you are the best," I said.

Olga laughed. "Thanks, sweetie," she said.

I looked over at her gleaming car.

"Think you could teach me to drive sometime?" I asked.

"In that?" she said, pointing at her car.

"Yeah," I said.

"Not on your life," she said.

The end

About the Author

Jürgen Banscherus is a worldwide phenomenon. There are almost a million Klooz books in print, and they have been translated into Spanish, Danish, Thai, Chinese, and eleven other languages. He has worked as a newspaper writer, a research scientist, and a teacher. His first book for children was published in 1985. He lives with his family in Germany.

About the Illustrator

Ralf Butschkow was born in Berlin. He works as a freelance graphic designer and illustrator, and has published more than 50 books for children. Critics have praised his work as "thoroughly enjoyable," "creatively original," and "highly recommended."

Glossary

bristle (BRISS-uhl)—a stiff brush, or the stiff hairs found on a brush

chrome (KROHM)—a shiny metal found on cars, often used as a decoration

roadblock (ROHD-blok)—an obstacle, something in your way

shift (SHIFT)—a certain time that you have to be working, or at your job

touch-up (TUTCH-up)—repair, clean, or fix

Discussion Questions

1. Do you think Klooz was brave or foolish to watch the car wash at night by himself? Why?

2. Why didn't Klooz tell the police about Steve and the screwdriver?

3. Olga made Steve pay to repaint all the cars that had been scratched. Do you think that was enough punishment? Why or why not?

Writing Prompts

1. Klooz got paid two hundred dollars for solving the car wash mystery. He plans to save it toward buying a computer. What would you do with the money?

2. Klooz thinks about the mystery while sitting in the bathtub and chewing gum. Do you have a special place or something you do when you want to solve a problem? Describe where you go and what you do when you need to relax and think about things.

3. You're trapped in a car wash! Describe what it's like. How does it smell, feel, sound? How did you get trapped, and how do you escape?

Internet Sites

Do you want to know more about subjects related to this book? Or are you interested in learning about other topics? Then check out FactHound, a fun, easy way to find Internet sites.

Our investigative staff has already sniffed out great sites for you!

Here's how to use FactHound:

1. Visit *www.facthound.com*

2. Select your grade level.

3. To learn more about subjects related to this book, type in the book's ISBN number: **1598893378**.

4. Click the **Fetch It** button.

FactHound will fetch the best Internet sites for you!